JANE

A Novella

Ash Ericmore

Written by: Ash Ericmore

Copyright © 2022 Ash Ericmore

ISBN: 9798739058751

CHAPTER 1

There was the guy that had just come out of the station. He had a determined gait to his walk. Short sleeved shirt. Blue suit trousers. Glasses. Looked like he had just come off shift at some teaching hospital. He walked straight by the taxi and crossed the street.

He got into a car parked on the other side of the road and kissed the girl sat in there waiting for him. Gordon had been watching her earlier. Watching her surreptitiously, wondering if she was the one. She had that mousey blond hair that always looked kind of dirty, but probably wasn't. She wasn't wearing makeup, but it was only five in the morning so she probably had just gotten out of bed to come and pick this schmuck up. Still, *he* seemed happy. There was a laugh, a touch, and then the engine started, the lights went on, and they pulled away.

Gordon returned his look to the doorway of the station. *Oh, come on*, he thought. There had to be some business this morning. He'd gotten here just before four so that he could catch anyone getting off the paper train. Sure, there was that one kid who looked about sixteen and was clearly coming down from something that he had taken last night, but no. He was a walker. Came out of the station and lit a fag the first chance he got. Staggered a bit, too. He weaved his way off in the direction of the town. Probably looking for the first opening café. Somewhere he could get his head—and his story—straight before heading home to his folks, sitting there wondering why little Johnny hadn't come home last night from the concert that he went to with his friends. Gordon smiled to himself. That was probably some nasty gig in Brixton, that he went to on his own, met some nonce that plied him with bad weed—or E, if he was lucky—and now he finds his way home on the paper train with no memory whatsoever of what happened last night. And odd bits of him hurt. But he probably believes the band were good.

Might not even have played.

Who knows?

The kid stumbled in the road, putting his hand out as if to stop a car that wasn't there from hitting him, before stooping down to retrieve the cigarette that he dropped and thrust it back into his mouth.

Maybe ... Gordon had shook his head and once again turned back to the station. *No.* Enough of thoughts like that. Let him go about his business.

The rumble of another train shook through the seat of his pants and snapped Gordon back to the here and now. He arched his back to look out to the side of the station building. The lights of train carriages came into view and slowed, as it got nearer the platform. It was a passenger train from London by the look of it. First one of the day. There wasn't much need of commuter trains from London to here. Birchingate—a rundown seaside town on the ghost-coast of Kent. No jobs here. But still they ran, and still they carried people. A few weeks ago Gordon had picked up a young woman from this very train. She came out of the station looking like she was just getting out of the shower. Dressed very inappropriately for travel. Too much skin and not enough clothing. She had a shoulder bag, one of those massive things that look like they can hold the kitchen sink and the bath as well. Flip flops. Can you fucking believe it? She came straight over and got in the taxi before Gordon had found time to turn off the passenger sign on the roof and gotten into the backseat without so much as a question. Gordon was left a little gobsmacked, to be honest.

She slung her bag in first, and slumped half naked onto the seat. "Beach," she had said. Not even a *please*. It was barely light, too. Gordon wasn't interested in the fare, but he wanted even less to start anything by trying to tell her he couldn't take her, so he turned the engine over and drove down the high street to the bottom of the hill and pulled to a stop. It wasn't more than a mile and she could have walked it in minutes, but he guessed that she wanted to get in early and get a spot.

Stupid sunbathers.

He'd charged her four pounds fifty, and when the look on her face changed, realising how expensive it was, he just added on the end, *minimum fare*. She looked plenty pissed but had started to dig around in her bag by that point anyway, so he turned back and returned his focus to the road. It was empty. You couldn't see the beach from there, you had to go down an alleyway and then down a flight of stairs to get to the beach, but it was just after five in the morning. It was going to be empty. She thrust a fiver at him over the seat and left her hand there, hanging, waiting for change. The cheek. He slipped her fifty pence and she got out without another word, slamming the door. He remembered thinking that he really ought to find out what the minimum fare was, because at some point someone was going to challenge him.

He still hadn't found out. He must do that.

The doors of the station opened, and Gordon watched to see if there might be any takers. The first one out was some geezer in a suit. Looked about thirty, but judging by the bulk under the tight fabric he could have been older. He looked like he spent too long in the gym. Had one of those military haircuts and hadn't shaved. Probably called all the girls in the club darling and all the boys son before trying to nail the seventeen year old that had gotten in with a dodgy ID.

Gordon rested his finger near the passenger light switch, ready to flick it off. He didn't want the fare.

But the geezer half-heartedly held the door for someone behind him. It was a woman. She strode out with purpose behind him. He let the door go just a split second too early, as if to appear polite, but actually got a win in his mind. One over on her. He had probably tried it on when they were on the train together and she'd shot him down.

Well, that's how it worked out in Gordon's mind, anyway.

He moved his finger a little away from the switch. The geezer was walking away from the door, still in his direction and the last thing he wanted or needed was to let this guy get the idea into his head that he was getting in the back. But equally … he looked by him to the woman.

She was a different story.

And there was no way that he was letting her go. Gordon watched her. She took the door in her stride, catching it as if she half expected this douche-canoe to drop it in her face, and then she came out behind him, letting the door go herself and looking up and down the car park. Was she looking for someone? That would be a shame. A real shame. *Maybe,* Gordon thought, *just maybe she's looking for a taxi.*

He withdrew his hand from the switch entirely. He had to take his chance with the guy. He was still striding like hc owned the place, trying to look bigger than he was. And now *she* had seen Gordon's passenger light and let out a little smile and started towards him.

Gordon's eyes flicked from the guy to the woman and back again. He was praying silently that this insufferable prick didn't open the rear door of the car. What could he do if he did? He'd have to take the fare and lose the girl. And that would suck balls.

He bit his lip as the guy came up level with the car and he closed his eyes. If there was a God, please, he'd never asked for anything before—he'd never ask for anything again—just let this arrogant, stupid looking, jacked-up, dickwad pass on by.

Gordon waited.

Waited.

Nothing happened. No door. No sound. No dickwad.

Gordon opened his eyes and looked in the passenger side wing mirror. He could see dickwad's arse wiggling down the little hill to the main road.

Half had a heart attacked when the woman pulled the door open and slid in. She dropped her arse down onto the seat first and then slid her legs in. Proper lady-like. Gordon looked in the mirror. He could see her lips. Deep red. Her mouth looked expensive.

She closed the door with a light click. The gentle touch.

"Where can I take you?" Gordon turned the engine over before flicking the passenger light off. He looked back into the mirror at her lips. She pulled the belt across the front of her.

"Rochester Road," she said. "L.J. Forts, and Sons." Her voice was sex line operator smooth. He immediately knew why dickwad had thrown his hat in the ring.

Gordon nodded. He knew Rochester Road well. It was the main drag between a couple of the larger towns in the district. Not far from here. Twenty minutes at most. He dropped the car into reverse and pulled it around in the car park, driving down to the main road and turning right. There wasn't any real traffic at this time. He saw dickwad looking through the window of a closed newsagent. Loser.

"You meeting someone there?" Gordon asked as he drove up to a stop on a set of traffic lights.

"I have questions that need answers and I wanted to do it in person."

Gordon looked at the clock on the dash. It was still only just after five-thirty. He frowned. "They opening up for you?"

"I didn't know how long it would take to get

there."

Gordon raised an eyebrow, and then twisted in his seat, raising his arm over the passenger seat to turn and look at her. "It's only going to take a few minutes," he said. "You'll be waiting on the street corner for a couple of hours like some hooker." He looked down her body. She didn't look like a hooker. She was … perfect.

"Green," she said.

He returned his eyes to her face. "Huh?"

"The lights have turned green."

Gordon stared at her for a second and then shuffled back around in his seat. "Right," he said, dropping the car into gear. "I was just saying that I would have you there in a few minutes, and perhaps you wouldn't want to stand on the street for a couple of hours."

"And what other activity do you suggest I partake in?"

She sounded posh, but not London posh. Gordon couldn't quite put his finger on where it was. It wasn't northern. That wouldn't do, anyway. He would have just dumped her on Rochester and headed back to the station. It wasn't foreign either. It was on the tip of his tongue. "Look, there's a nice café on Rochester. *Bean There*." He chuckled to himself. Got him every time. "Geddit?" He glanced in the mirror in time to catch her ryely raise the corner of her mouth.

"Very good," she said quietly. "Fine. As long as they sell coffee."

Gordon shook his head. "What café don't sell

coffee?" He let the question hang. He wasn't really expecting an answer anyway. He took the first left at the next roundabout and went by ASDA—the car park was deserted. "I remember when that was twenty-four hour." If he didn't keep up the banter she'd get suspicious. Left at the next roundabout and through a housing estate to a set of traffic lights. "This is Rochester Road," he said, glancing back at her mouth. The lights changed and he turned left again.

Soon enough, *Bean There* was on the right and Gordon pulled over. He stopped outside and drummed his fingers on the steering wheel. "Huh." The café was shrouded in complete darkness. He scratched the back of his head, feigning confusion. "Well."

Bean There had been closed down three weeks ago by the Food Standards. The local rag had a Facebook page and on there they had reported that it had been closed down due to ongoing food preparation concerns. In the comments someone had said that they were there when a little old lady had seen a rat on the floor under the table. Someone else said that they spat in the food. Someone else had intimated something unsavoury about their mayonnaise. But whatever the reason, the FSA had stomped in wearing their jack boots and closed the place down.

He turned in his seat. "Sorry, Love. They appear to be closed." He looked at her again and tried his most pitiful face. "Look," he said. "I only live around the corner. I have coffee." He nodded towards the houses. "I live on the estate. I feel like I led you astray. How about you come back to my place and have a coffee—no extra charge."

She frowned and sucked air in through her mouth and then breathed it out through her nose as she stared at back at him. He couldn't read the look and thought she might say no. *Banter your way out of it, man.* "No funny business mind," he continued. "I'm not that kind of boy."

She smiled and let out a small laugh.

It was sweet.

"Okay then. I'll try to restrain myself," she said.

He threw her a wink and twisted back to face front, pulling the car back out onto the empty road.

C H A P T E R   2

It was still not six in the morning and the car was idling in his driveway. Gordon turned the engine off and got out of the car. He waited to see if the woman was going to get out by herself or if she was going to wait for him to open the door like a common chauffeur. He tossed the keys in the air and caught them again without moving and that seemed to be all the indication that she needed.

The door opened from the inside and the woman got out carrying the purse and document case she had with her. Gordon smiled warmly. This was the first time he had been able to look at her without having his view interrupted. She was slender, but not thin. Had on a business suit—dark purple. She had dark red hair. Gordon was a simple man, and he liked what he saw. She was just right.

He turned back to the house and went over and opened the front door. Listening, he could hear her follow.

"You have a nice house," she said, gaining ground on him as he fingered the keys.

He did, yes. The estate itself was tawdry. It had been a shitty council estate in the sixties and sold off, piece meal, in the eighties. *The Newingstairs Estate.* It had a rep. Largely, it was row upon row of organised two up, two downs with small back gardens and even smaller front ones. Most of the front ones had been turned into driveways just long enough to get a Fiesta on there or some other trash heap that cost less than a grand and probably had no tax, or insurance in it. Most of them probably didn't know what an MOT was.

It was a haven of the unemployed. Drug addicts. Kid factories. All playing the local job centre for as much benefit as they could screw out of them.

But Gordon's house was different. A few years back he had secured the property in a nice little deal for a good price. No one wanted to live there. Surrounded by … this. It was the last house in the close and detached. The only one like it. It had a large front garden when he'd bought it with a garage to the side. He had quickly converted the garden into a drive in, drive out, driveway. Super posh, like. He rarely found the need to use the garage these days, but he could still pull in there and work on the car if he needed to.

The house was double fronted and rendered, painted white. Compared to the rest of the street—with kiddies trikes discarded to the side of the road and even the stereotypical sofa in the front garden in one house—it was a mansion.

"Keeps the rain off," he said, smiling to himself. He opened the door and stood to the side to allow the woman to pass him. She stepped in through the front door and he took his opportunity to drop his nose as close to her as he dare and take a whiff. The perfume wasn't cheap. But not to his taste.

But it would wash off.

Gordon held his keys up towards the car and pressed the button. The dark blue Mondeo beeped once as it locked and then he followed her into the house and closed the door behind her. She stood in the hallway at the bottom of the stairs clutching her bag in front of her. Gordon smiled and held his hand up to guide her into the kitchen: through the door to the back of the house.

She obliged and Gordon followed her through, gently closing the kitchen door behind them and waving her over to the table, to sit.

"Thank you," she said, taking her seat. "My name is Jane." She tagged the words on with a tick of uncomfortableness in her voice.

"How rude of me." Gordon turned to the kettle and flipped it on. "Gordon. It's nice to meet you." He took the few steps across the kitchen and to the table and thrust his hand towards her. She took it. She had a firm grip. "So what do you do?" he asked, turning back to the cabinets and busying himself with making coffee.

She started saying something about increasing annual blah-blah, but Gordon tuned out. He got down a couple of mugs and spooned in some Nescafe. "Milk and sugar?" He interrupted her.

She stopped talking for a second, thrown from her spiel. "Oh, yes. One please." She was quiet for only a couple of seconds before starting up again.

Gordon picked up a sugar cube with his fingers from the open bowl of them on the counter and dropped one into her mug. Then he took the milk from the waist high fridge next to the sink and slopped some in. Again, only into her mug. Then he opened the cutlery drawer and took out a spoon and a tablet, dropping both of them into her mug.

Click.

The kettle rumbled as the water rolled, and turned itself off. Gordon filled both of the mugs and stirred them. He took hers over to the table and placed it in front of her, and then retreated to his on the counter. It was best to stay a safe, passive, distance from her. He didn't want to be too forward, or too confining. He didn't want to spook her. He leaned against the counter and lifted his own coffee to his lips and blew on it before sipping.

It was good. Black. Strong.

Jane picked her coffee up and tasted it. Only a little. She was probably testing the heat. She smiled over the lip of the mug before taking more.

Gordon raised his arm, coffee in hand. "Cheers," he said, before placing his mug down and coming over to the table. He pulled the chair out and sat opposite her. "Family?" He must have taken her aback. She seemed surprised. She immediately moved her right hand over her left as if to cover where she might have a ring on. She didn't. Gordon had already checked.

"No." She paused for a moment. "Well, parents, and such." She waved a little dismissively. "But no husband … boyfriend."

Gordon lost focus for a second and let his eyes flick down to her hands, tearing them from hers, and then returning them in an instant. It didn't feel right. If she was without a man in her life, why did she instinctively cover her ring fingers? And she noticed him doing it, too. *Damn*.

"I divorced a while back," she said. She seemed to relax and parted her hands, concentrating them on the mug instead.

She's lying. Gordon smiled. *Double damn.* If only he hadn't looked. The last thing he needed was to have to wonder what were lies, and what was not.

"Trouble in paradise." She said it with a slight slur. As she spoke she squinted, focussing on the mug she held just away from her face. She placed it down, the colour draining from her a little.

Gordon looked at the mug. *Good.* He didn't want to have to clean up the coffee if she dropped it. He looked up to her face and she was looking at him, lips pursed.

"What have you done?" she asked. She spoke slowly. Deliberately.

Gordon shrugged. "What have I?"

She blinked once, twice, thrice. And then her eyelids dropped slowly. She tried to raise her arms, Gordon could see her thinking about flailing. Thinking about escape, but there was none of that. And then her head slumped forward.

"Jane?" he asked, eyebrow raised. He patted her on the back of the hand. Nothing Zip. She was out. Gordon stood and took her coffee to the sink, pouring the remains out. It wouldn't do to get the cups mixed up later. He was going to need some sort of refreshment when he'd finished and taking a gulp of her stone cold coffee wasn't going to make the situation better.

He set her mug down in the sink and opened the kitchen door, and then to the right and under the stairs, the door to the basement. He flipped the light on and looked down the staircase to the lower floor. Wooden stairs with smooth concrete walls went down to a screed covered floor. He checked the ceiling for spiders. He hated spiders, and they always seemed to find their way to the basement, no matter how securely locked down it was.

He returned to the kitchen and weighed up Jane. He wanted to carry her down there, but wasn't sure if she was going to prove too heavy. The last thing he had wanted to do was drop her. That could kill her there and then, and nobody wanted that. *Maybe easier to drag her*, he thought.

He got around behind her and took her weight, placing his hands under her shoulders into her armpits and pulled. The chair tumbled to the side and he dragged her through the kitchen. It was easy enough. Smooth tiled floor. Out in the hallway it was a little harder. It was a cheap shag, but the carpet put up some resistance. He backed through the doorway onto the stairs and dragged her. It wasn't easy going down backwards while trying not to brain her, but it was better than pulling her down by her feet, her head slapping against every step. He stopped halfway to regain his breath and checked his watch. The Rohypnol would last plenty.

He got to the bottom of the steps and lowered her gently to the floor, before opening the door to her room.

Once secured in the room, Gordon dropped to the chair by the door and took a few minutes to regain his breath.

When he'd bought the house, the basement was

the same size footprint as the house—give or take. It was completely open plan and left for storage. As soon as he'd seen it, when the snotty estate agent had shown him around, he knew then, it was perfect.

Shortly after moving in, he'd bought a drum kit.

Gordon didn't like the idea of wasting money, but this was a long con, and was going to be worth it. He set the thing up in the basement and banged at it for a while. Honestly, he'd thought it was going to be easy. Bang this one like this, knock that one every other time, tap his foot. But it was hard. Like incomprehensibly hard.

But all the better he supposed.

And he continued like that for a few weeks.

Every night, sometimes with a day in between, he'd go down into the basement and bang the shit out of the drums for as long as his stamina would allow.

The neighbours hated it.

The whole damned street could hear him.

Then he called in some trades and had the basement converted. He had the space split into three. At the bottom of the stairs there was a small area for storage—he had a large chest freezer there for convenience—then into a second room—for the band, with a small bathroom off of it, toilet and shower, for further convenience.

And then had the whole lot sound proofed.

Once everyone was happy, the trades finished and paid, and the neighbours convinced he'd done it so as to be a good fellow, he moved the drum kit up into the attic—vowing never to touch the Godforsaken thing again—and turned the band room into a bedroom. He changed the locks on the door to be high security with the help of some Youtube videos, and when he had the new furniture delivered for the "spare bedroom" he lugged it all downstairs and furnished the room.

One last job, and it was a tricky one, but he secured an iron clasp to the wall and concreted it in. Somewhere a chain could be attached.

He looked around the room now, all complete and even decorated in a light purple, and was happy with the renovation. His eyes dropped to Jane, lying on the bed, a large steel ring around her ankle with a chain that connected her to the wall.

The chain was long enough to allow her access to the bathroom, as well as the bed, TV, and the table and chair, but she couldn't reach the wall where he sat now, his chair, or the door.

He looked at his watch. She would still be asleep for hours and he was tired after the workout. He stretched his back and stood, going out of the door and closing it and bolting it behind him. It had a small window at head height that he could still see her from, and he'd fitted a small blind to it, so it could be drawn down and she wouldn't be able to see out.

He pulled the blind down, covering the eight inch square window, and went upstairs. He closed the door to the basement, and made a sandwich in the kitchen.

He'd barely taken a bite when he found himself starting to think about sleep more than anything else, so he went upstairs and got into bed. It was just gone eight when he closed his eyes and drifted away.

Gordon dreamt of something strange in the darkness. As he woke, his eyes still closed, he could see the creatures moving in the shadows. He clenched his eyes together to try and shake the strange sick feeling that came with the waves of movement still going on behind his eyelids. He opened his eyes and waited for a moment for them to focus. The light was bright, so bright. He must have left the curtains open—of course, it was still early morning when he turned in and he must have been asleep for some hours.

He blinked away the sleep.

He stared straight forward, looking out of the window of the Mondeo. He was behind the wheel, in the driver's seat, with his seat belt on. Both of his hands were on the steering wheel, locked almost in a death grip. He forced his fingers apart, and they made a suckering sound as they released the leather of the wheel.

What the fuck?

He looked out of the side window. The car was parked raggedly on the side of a narrow road, with cornfields on each side.

What the fuck? he thought, again.

He looked at his watch, noticing the red goo that was over the palms of this hands. It was sticky. It must have been what was keeping his hands on the wheel. Jesus. It was disgusting. He flicked his hands, wringing them to try and dislodge it all. Goo and bits of gross shit. *Jesus.* He looked at the time. It was four in the afternoon. Gordon went to pinch his nose and stopped himself as the goo covered hand got close. He could smell it, too.

"Bits of fucking …" He stopped himself. What had he done? He didn't remember. He was at home. He put Jane to bed and then he went to the kitchen. He was tired. Went upstairs for a nap. Then what? "… person goo." He looked back out of the windscreen … and where the fuck was he?

He opened his seatbelt and flipped it off him, leant over to the glove box and dropped it open. It has a packet of baby wipes for emergencies. *Or KFC*, he shrugged, pulling one from the top of the pack and half wiping and half scraping at the people goo on his hands. He used a couple of wipes, getting most of it off, before tossing them to the passenger foot well, and opening the door. He got out and stood by the car for a second. There was nothing coming. Nothing had gone by him since he woke up, in fact.

He stepped out into the centre of the road and looked around. There was a large factory looking building in the distance. It could have been the one on the way out of town. No way to know from here. But if it was he hadn't gone far.

He jumped back in behind the wheel and started the engine, pulling out onto the road, and driving in the general direction of the factory.

Maybe he'd drugged himself in the kitchen, he pondered as he drove. He'd never done it before. The women never sleep walked when they were drugged. But he *was* a man. Drug-induced sleep-driving. It was possible. He looked at his hands. But drug-induced what else?

He reached a crossing soon enough and saw that it was in fact the factory from just outside town and that he was maybe thirty minutes' drive from the house.

He wondered what he was going to find when he got there.

C H A P T E R   4

Gordon drove along Rochester Road casually, but kept an eye on his surroundings. He didn't know what he'd done, and that was fine if he'd just done something to Jane. She was, after all, secured securely, and soundproofed, at home. But if he'd done something to someone else … it could mean anything. He watched for police activity. Made sure no one was following him.

He drove along the side of the supermarkets and went right at the first set of lights. Taking the back road onto the estate. It would be safer in case anyone was waiting for him. Might give him a chance. He pulled up at the next set of traffic lights and waited, drumming his fingers lightly on the wheel. He gotten back long after the schools had turned out and the traffic was light.

"Oh, shit," he said to himself. He dragged the seat belt off and reached down into the foot well, grabbing the wipes covered in bits of someone. He lowered the window, gave a quick check out of the window to make sure the pigs weren't watching him and then tossed them out into the gutter.

The lights changed and Gordon continued.

He didn't see anyone out of the ordinary between the lights and the house. He drew into the driveway and turned the engine off. Waited. He kept watch in the rear view mirror half expecting a ton of police cars to follow him, cornered, into the close.

Five minutes went by and nothing.

He slowly opened the car door and got out.

"Gordo!" The voice came from across the street. In his haste to ensure he wasn't about to snagged by the fuzz, he hadn't thought to check to make sure Nathan, from two doors down, wasn't in the garden. Nathan was a tosser.

"Shit," he muttered to himself. He looked over to Nathan, standing in his front garden. Nathan's garden was all roses. The guy was unemployed—one of those layabouts that sponges off the state claiming for just about anything when he was just suffering from nothing more than twatitice and terminal laziness. And he spent too much of the unemployment green on fucking roses and his stupid yappy Chihuahua. In fact, if the police did come around the corner now, Gordon had mind to take Nathan out with him. "Evening," he called back, out loud.

Nathan waved half-heartedly, and then waved the tiny shovel he was hold towards the Mondeo. "You have a leak," he called.

Gordon walked to the back of the car and looked down. Deep red goo was coming from the back of the car and dripping onto his pristine driveway. *Fuck. Fuck. Fuck.* He glanced back to Nathan to make sure the nosey fucker wasn't coming to *help*, before he popped the boot open.

"Shit."

He quickly looked over to Nathan and nodded with a smile. "Tin of paint," he called. "Lids popped off." He shook his head feigning some sort of exasperation, and waved his hands out. "What you gonna do?" He slammed down the boot and walked calmly over to the garage, slipping his key in the lock and opening the shutter. It was tidy enough inside, and there was plenty of room to pull the car in.

He returned to the car and drove it up, into the garage. He wasn't concerned with it dripping in the garage—there was a handy soak away in the floor, and what dripped in the garage wouldn't come out under the shutter. We went back outside and dropped the shutter. Gordon didn't need this. He looked at the goo on the drive. This was going to smell soon enough and draw in some flies.

He sighed.

Going around the back of the house he turned on the hose and washed down the drive as casually as he could, even giving a polite wave to Nathan, begrudgingly. The gloop ran down the drive and into the gutter probably easier than actual paint, and that was something, at least.

When he'd finished he slung the hose to the side by the fence and retreated to the front door of the house and in. *What a day.* He pinched the top of this nose and went to the kitchen. Looking at the cup on the side and the sandwich he had started on. *Something* had drugged him. He tossed the sandwich in the bin and dropped the door of the dishwasher open. "Oh, for fuck's sake," he blurted out. It was full of clean dishes. He took a cup from the top and put it next to the kettle, poured the water from the kettle down the sink, and then refilled it. He started a sterile cup of coffee.

He then unloaded the dishwasher, and reloaded it.

This wasn't the day he was expecting at four this

morning. He should be playing with his new toy by now. He paused and thought about the car. It would be fine until tomorrow, wouldn't it?

But it would dry up.

Maybe he had time to just stick his head in on Jane and see how she was doing?

The kettle rumbled and clicked. He poured himself a fresh coffee, putting both sugar and milk in it this time. He took a sip. He'd go down and chat with Jane for a few minutes and then go and clean up the car. Yes. That was the way forward.

It was slightly worrying that he'd completely spaced the morning. He might even have enjoyed it. He put the cup down and went downstairs.

C H A P T E R 5

Gordon raised the blind and looked through the window into Jane's room. He frowned. She was standing there in the centre of the room like a mannequin. He shook his head, hoping she wasn't some loony.

He pushed the bolt back, drew his warmest smile on his face, and unlocked the door, pulling it open.

She looked up.

"Jane." He drew his hands out warmly, but didn't approach her. He glanced quickly to her ankle where he could see she was still perfectly restrained. "How did you sleep?"

She stared at him. The look on her face was something. He'd seen worse given the situation. The last lass was a screamer. One of the reasons it didn't work out. All she'd do is moan at him. *Moan, moan, moan. Let me out. Yadda, yadda.* But she was younger, he supposed. Kids today don't know what they've got when they've got it. Jane on the other hand looked put out, but not *pissed* as such. But she didn't speak.

Gordon let his hands down to his side and dropped onto the chair by the door. The one she couldn't reach. He smiled at her. "You look smashing," he said.

"Where is my food?" she asked. She enunciated clearly, and spoke slowly, like she was talking to a child.

Gordon looked at his watch. Hm, it *was*

dinnertime, he supposed, and he was a little peckish himself, what with all the sleep murder. He slapped his hands flatly on his knees and pushed himself up, before stopping himself. "Huh," he said, returning his look to her. "I think you mean, *can I please have something to eat*. You could even add *Master* on the end. If you wanted pudding, like."

"The flesh," she said. "Feed me the flesh."

"And a-what now?" Gordon raised his eyebrows and dropped back onto the chair. "I think you're getting ahead of yourself young lady." *Young*, he thought to himself.

"You have brought me a child. Feed me the flesh."

Gordon frowned. *How could …?* "What do you know about that then?" He leaned forward in the chair.

"If you do not bring me the flesh willingly, you will do it unwillingly."

Gordon sucked in his cheeks. This was taking a turn. He scratched his face. "I can't yet. The child is in the garage and I can't get the child into the house until it is properly dark." *That's right, humour her.* That said, he could harbour the body in the storeroom freezer for a few days. Until he worked out where he'd gotten it from. He didn't know if it was a he or she. It was goo.

"Do it now," she said.

"Okay, love." Gordon stood and left the room closing the door behind him. He locked the door, bolted it, and stared at Jane as he pulled the blind down. "What on earth," he muttered to himself, returning to the ground floor and the kitchen. He pulled out a roll of bin liners from under the sink and pulled one from it. He held it out. It looked like he might be able to fit the child's corpse in there. It was pretty messed up and probably quite pliable. He reached into the cupboard and got a pair of marigolds, dragging them onto his hands like surgical gloves, releasing the elasticity with a satisfying *pluck*.

So, whatever this silly woman's game was, he would call her bluff. Dump the corpse in the middle of the room. Give her a shoulder to cry on when she realised what she had asked for, and then put the damn thing in the freezer for a couple of days. Then she could clean the floor up.

Perfect.

He took the bin liner and left through the back door, rounding the side of the house and going into the garage through the side door. As soon as he closed the door he could hear the flies. Blue bottles, their incessant low hum overtaking all other sounds in the confined room—even the sound of his own breathing.

The garage was stuffy. Uncomfortably so, with it being quite a warm day, from what he could actually remember of the day. He flipped the light on and went to rear of the car, pressing the key fob to unlock it. Took in a long, deep breath. Opened the boot.

A handful of flies took out into the room, fleeing for the sudden light, swarming around Gordon. He was already hot, sweating, all due to the lack of air in the room. And now the smell. It was a rancid, chemical-like smell. A bad butcher's shop at opening time on a hot day type smell. Been in the boot since this morning, and the flies had been picking it apart.

Gordon looked at it. It was probably the size of a black sack when it could have stood up. That would have made it, what, three foot tall? Six year old, maybe? Tee shirt on the top, by the look of it. Maybe a boy, but who could make that sort of assumption these days? Pair of shorts on the bottom. The kid was lying face down. It'd shit itself, of that there was no doubt. The tee was probably yellow. There was a small patch on the back at the base that wasn't stained a deep mahogany from all the dried blood. Shorts could have been any colour. Just mahogany now. The kid didn't have and shoes or socks on.

Maybe he'd picked it up at the beach?

He went to reach down and roll the body over when he noticed there was a knife nestled up against the wall of the boot. He took it by the handle. The blade was covered in crusted blood, the handle caked. He examined it a little closer. It was his, from the kitchen. He was certainly sloppy when he was sleep murdering. *Taking his own kitchen knife.* He shook his head and tossed it back onto the floor of the boot.

Gordon sighed and took a deep breath—him getting used to the smell and all. He grabbed the body by the shoulder and yanked it over. It was like a plaster, you see. Best to get it over with. The head was still attached, just. Which was just as well, because that sort of thing was enough to make even him a wee bit jumpy. It was a boy. *Yes,* he thought, *probably six or seven.* It looked like he'd taken the knife to the kid's throat to shut him up and hacked away a little too many times. He stuck his fingers in the gash and snorted a little laugh. The body was still warm, kept to a nice temperature by the heat of the garage. The knife had gone deep. He was no doctor, but he could feel through to the larynx and wiggled his fingers down into the trachea. Because of the warmth, the blood was still fluid, and rigor hadn't set in yet.

Good.

He looked at the bin liner. "Damn it." It was going to be like trying to get a rose bush in there without any help. Push one bit in and another bit would flop out. Rigor might have helped, if the kid was at the right angle. *Never mind*, he thought. He dropped the bin liner over the body and took a step back. Yep, it was going to fit.

Gordon picked up the bin liner and fed it over the kid's head, sliding it under like he was putting on a duvet cover. Gordon was a *mother fucking God* at putting on duvet covers. He slid the bag down to the kids legs and lifted.

"Fuck it." The bag ripped. Gordon picked up the knife and sliced it repeatedly into the kids corpse. "Fuckitfuckitfuckit." He slammed the knife in one last time. "And *fuck you*." He left the garage slamming the door behind him and returning the kitchen, careful to leave the marigolds on the corpse. No sense in making more mess than he needed to.

He got the whole roll of bags this time. He returned to the car and dragged the body out of the boot, letting sloop onto the floor, letting out some of the stench of shit. "Fuck sake." It was starting to piss him off. This had better be worth it. *She'd* better be worth it.

He unrolled the bags but didn't tear them off, leaving them in a long sheet. He dropped them to the floor and carefully wrapped the kid in them like a rug. The oldies are always the best. Roll it in a rug.

He scooped the body up and returned to the house, kicking the door of the garage closed behind him and not stopping in the kitchen. The roll was *overly persistent* in the dripping department. He got to the bottom of the stairs and rested the gooey, dripping, wretched parcel on the top of the freezer, bits of blood coagulating almost instantly on the lid of the freezer and the smell of shit filling the small space.

"Oh, God fucking damn."

He unlocked the door and released the bolt, pulling the blind up and peering through before he opened it. There was no way in Hell that she was going to have gotten free (and if she had he was going to be having words with the hardware counter down at B & Q), but it was better to be safe than sorry.

She was still standing in the middle of the room, but now she was grinning somewhat maniacally. It caused Gordon a moment of pause. What was she up to? He opened the door and poked his head in. "Hi."

"Where is the flesh?" she asked. "I can …" She pulled a long breath in through her nose. "… smell it."

"It's just here." He looked her up and down. "You are a strange one. You sure you're ready for this?"

She nodded without word.

Gordon stuck his bottom lip out and shrugged. "Fine." He returned to the freezer and picked up the boy in his arms, cradling him like a baby. Or a ham. He walked it into the room sideways like he was carrying his bride across the threshold, unlike the way he had dragged Jane in there herself, only hours ago. "Your *flesh* smells like shit." He tried as hard as he could to keep his nose away from *the package*, but there was no hiding the ripe stench of soiled pants.

"Put it there." She pointed to the floor in front of her. She wasn't at the full length of the chain and was asking that the boy be put well within reach of her.

Gordon was well aware that she would also be able to reach him if he were to put the body down there, but he was willing to take that risk just to see how this played out. He knelt down and rested the body wrapped in plastic on the floor. "You're sure about this?" He stood, but didn't back away. "So are you going to tell me how you did it?"

Her grin faltered, but didn't drop. Her eyes never left the black plastic wrapping. "What?"

"This macabre magic trick? How did you know I'd been … sleep murdering?"

"Because I told you too." Finally she looked up to him. "Leave us." She pointed to the door.

Stranger and stranger. Gordon shrugged. "Your funeral."

"Go and clean up," she said. "I won't be long."

It crossed Gordons mind that maybe she was sicker in the head than he was. Sure, he'd stopped taking the medication that was supposed to help him about three years ago when he moved out of London and came down here, changing his name and everything, but that hadn't had an effect on his behaviour. He thought. But he was fairly sure that he was different to other people. Maybe she was like him?

Maybe this *would* work out.

But he couldn't help but feel a little uncomfortable. He backed towards the door, watching her. He couldn't quite make her out.

Gordon bumped into the doorframe, before going out into the storeroom. He pushed the door closed and bolted it, watching through the window.

She never moved. Not an inch. She just watched him, waiting. Smiling.

Gordon pulled the blind down. He breathed, for the first time in a few minutes. That was weird. Really fucking weird.

He turned back to the bloodied freezer and started to tidy up.

C H A P T E R   6

Sometime later, as the sun had dropped from the sky and the streetlights were on, Gordon hosed down the boot of the car. The gore ran through the drainage holes—as Gordon liked to call them, they were rust holes really—and down into the garage's soak away. He was subconsciously humming a Sex Pistols and tapping his foot. The smell of death in the garage was dissipating slowly.

When satisfied, Gordon rolled the hose around his arm, wending his way from the garage to the back of the house and dumping it on the path. He went back and locked up the car, the garage, and the back door before returning to the basement to see Jane.

He stood there, wondering for a moment what to expect, before opening the blind and looking through into the room. Jane was sitting on the edge of the bed now. She was wearing the dressing gown that he had left on the back of the bathroom door, and nothing else besides. Her hair was wet.

Gordon frowned.

He looked around the floor. The body was gone, and in its place was pooling blood, and strange looking detritus. Lumps and clumps of things that weren't there before. Without looking from her, he fumbled around to unbolt the door and only looked away once he had the doorknob in his hand. He opened the door and went in, only so far as to the safety of the chair at the door. He didn't sit. Stood, he looked from her to the bloodied floor and back again. "Body in the bathroom, is it?" he asked, somewhat confused.

She was fiddling with her hair and a towel. "No." She didn't look up to him.

Gordon had had enough. He took the opportunity given by the fact that she was *busy with her hair* and stormed across the room to the bathroom. The room was wet, and clean. He stuck his head over the bath and aside from a ring of residue, there was no signs of the body … just some blood.

He turned back from the bathroom and looked at her, still prettying herself. "What is this, some kind of magic trick?" She didn't respond. He stalked over to the bed where she was sat, crouched and flipped the sheets up to see under. Nothing. He looked at her again, and she showed no interest in him whatsoever. "Huh." He walked over to the mess on the floor. Bending down he poked at the things awash with blood. Clothing. But not the boy's. At least, not *just* the boy's. It was hers too, ripped to shreds. And weirdly the bin liners where untouched. Gordon hurried back over to the door.

The safety of the door.

"What the fuck is going on? What did you do? Can you get out?"

Jane looked up to him, still patting her hair with the towel. "I was hungry. I consumed the flesh. No. But I will require more sustenance. As you did not bring me sufficient."

Gordon shook his head. This had never happened before. Not once. Jesus fucking Christ. He grabbed a fucking looney, cannibal, nutter, and she seemed to be … enjoying herself. "I … I'm going to let you think about what you've done," he said, extremely unsure of himself for the first time in forever.

He backed out of the door and slammed it, hurriedly pushing the bolt across. Then he stood there, feeling a little safer as he watched her. She finished her hair without looking up at him and returned to the bathroom where she dropped off the towel. Then she returned to the bed and sat, leaning against the headboard with her eyes shut.

Was she going to sleep now? The cheek of it.

Gordon pulled the blind down, annoyed. Hm. Well … at least he didn't have to dispose of the body. Fucking psycho. Gordon returned to the ground floor and closed the door to the basement. He'd let her stew in her own juice for a little while. That'd teach her. He went into the living room and flopped on the sofa, pulling out his phone and opening the Just Eat app. He picked up the remote and flicked on the TV. Sitcom. He flipped to the next channel. Cookery show. Gordon only had Freeview. He thought that TV largely rotted the brain and didn't want the extra expense of Sky just to watch the cricket a few times a year. He looked back at the app. *Kebab?* he thought to himself. *Kebab.* He nodded.

He opened *Best Kebab and Pizza*. They had the *best*—forgive the pun—kebabs for delivery. It was still early enough for him not to get indigestion. He order the XL donor, salad, chilli sauce, and chips. That way he met the delivery price requirement. He pushed order, and the app told him it would be thirty to forty-five minutes. It would be early. Best was only just around the corner, and besides, he was a regular.

Gordon sat back in the sofa, letting the warm fluffiness of the cushions surround him. The kebab was good. A little sloppier than usual, but still good. It had belly-busted him, and the third can of extra strength imported lager he held had finished him off. Today was a bust for sure. Confusing, too. Still, he had Jane and that was a plus, even if she was a little strange. That said, if she proved too much, he could leave her down there for a week or two without going down. Out of sight, out of mind, so to speak. That would fix that.

But for today, he was done. He flipped the TV off. It was some American cop show CSI, forensics thing, that didn't seem to hold up, at least to here in the UK. They'd never gotten shit on him, right? These shows mush be fabricated.

He pulled and pushed himself from the sofa and stood, wapping his hand against his belly. "Bellies gonna getcha," he giggled to himself. He stopped outside the living room at the door to the basement. He had considered going down and seeing if she was okay (both literally, and figuratively) but decided against it. It was late. Tomorrow was another day.

CHAPTER 7

Gordon struggled to open his eyes. They were gummed together, like his eyes had watered in his sleep and glued them shut. "What the …" He knew before he had opened them that he wasn't in bed again. "*Nooooooo*," he whined, long and hard. He pinched at his eyelashes and rubbed his eyes until they opened. He was sitting on the ground. It was dark. He waited until his eyes accustomed themselves to the light, realizing then, that he was in the garage.

Thank fuck for that.

But this was no joke. Why had he started sleep walking? He got to his feet and before leaving the garage, noticed that he had blood on his hands again. "Really?" Sleep murder again? He turned to the car, staring at the boot. "And what surprises are in store today?" He popped the boot open.

Empty.

Right.

He left the garage and hurried over to the house. It was daylight. He had no idea what time. He wasn't wearing his watch, and he saw that the blood was on more than just his hands. He looked to be creamed in it like a shit wedding cake. He went in through the back door. The street had been empty, so it was probably still early. The only sign of stirring was Nathan's stupid dog yapping incessantly from over his way somewhere.

He went straight to the bathroom upstairs to wash. Getting there he saw that he was caked in more blood than he had imagined. It was all up in his face. Hair. Over his clothes. He looked like a deranged Red-Shirt. He smiled to himself. It *was* a good look, but … what the fuck was happening? Gordon stripped naked and jumped in the shower, washing every inch of himself. There wasn't just blood. Whatever he'd done to whoever he must have done a solid job. There was bits of brain in his hair. Bone fragments. Some too big to go down the plug hole. Once he'd cleaned himself, he stared at the pile of clothes and human bits that wouldn't go down the hole. He'd run out of bin liners. Well, there were some in the basement. And perhaps he should ask Jane WHAT THE FUCK WAS GOING ON for one last time.

Then there was the concern over the fact that he had killed someone, somehow, and he didn't know where the body was. *Well*, he thought to himself, *"probably" killed someone.*

Hurriedly dressing, Gordon made his way to the basement. He'd put on work jeans and a paint covered sweatshirt just in case he stumbled over a body on the way. He pulled the blind open. Jane was sitting on the bed, naked. He watched her for a moment. She hadn't noticed him, or if she had, she had made no attempt to cover her nakedness.

She had a decent body. Gordon would quite often have to force them to show him, so this was a pleasant change. He tried to judge how old she was. It was never easy to tell when someone was wearing makeup and dressed. She was maybe … thirty? A little older than his usual trophy, but still, she seemed to have plus points.

Gordon opened the door and entered, sitting

straight on the chair by the door. Jane made no attempt to cover her modesty. She sat there, on the bed, facing him. "Right young lady," he said, trying his hardest to be authoritarian about things. "What, and when, did you slip me a Jimmy? There's no way this is a coincidence."

"Of course not," she said, smiling like a mother pacifying her confused child. "I have not slipped you a *Jimmy*." She said the word Jimmy like she'd never heard the term before. "But it is me that is causing you to take outings to find me flesh. I did tell you that you would feed me, one way or the other."

Gordon shuffled on his chair. "Go on," he said, unsure. She must be cray-cray, obviously, but he didn't have any answers himself.

"Have you not noticed the influence that I can have over you? That I *have* had over you since you brought me down here. You do what I want, when I tell you. You rarely even question it. And in your dreams … in your dreams you are only my puppet."

"You're fucking crazy."

"I am not." She stood. "Do you want to see?"

"See what? You're not hiding much. Have you got something up your arse?"

Jane closed her eyes while Gordon watched. Uncertain, he didn't want to look away. She let a small smile come from her, her mouth widening slowly. There was a crack that cut through the air. Quiet at first, then loud. It was the sort of crack that made your teeth itch. She pulled her shoulders back a little. There was the crack again. It was coming from her. It was coming from inside her. Gordon tried to back away, but his feet felt like lead. "Jane," he said.

A line appeared on her chest, between her breasts.

Gordon could do nothing more than watch.

It grew, the length of the sternum, splitting slowly like a ripe peach, blood oozing slowly from the growing wound, at first, and then, the blood stopped. It wasn't natural. A split like that should have caused gushing.

Gordon tried again to move. His head was starting to ache. A migraine coming from nowhere.

The wound grew slowly, widening as if a retractor was in place. Puss started to sloop from the opening, and behind it, dark space. Nothing. The flesh weeped a bloody phlegm coloured goo, as the split grew in length. Dropping down to her belly and lower to her crotch.

Gordon raised his hand, cradling his head. His nose had started to run. He dragged his eyes from her split to her face. She still had her eyes closed, and yet he could somehow still feel her watching him. "What are you?" he whimpered, no more than a whisper.

"God," she said quietly. "I am *your* God."

The spilt continued down, and Jane reached into the split taking each side of it, holding the flesh in her hands, and she pulled. She pulled the wound open, showing him her inside, offering him herself to read like she was showing him a book.

"Why can't I move?" Gordon wasn't sure if he even said the words. They may have been in his head, or maybe even she had thought them for him. He looked inside her. He looked into the abyss that shouldn't have been there, the abyss that couldn't have been there. Inside Jane was an infinity, she had Heaven in there, Hell, stars. He wiped his nose with the back of his hand as the blood started to dribble into his mouth. He realised he was shaking. Sickness from his stomach rising as he stared uncontrollably at her. It. At everything she was. He tried, failing, to blink. His head growing light. The vomit rose in his throat, and he tried to swallow it back, but it reached his mouth, filling it with burning. He could feel the bile on his tongue, on his teeth, he could feel the heat on skin as it burned him. He tried to spit it away, but it drooled out of his mouth like he was no more in control of himself than an infant.

"I am hungry," she said.

Gordon lost control of his bowels. He felt the shit running down his leg, and then he blacked out.

CHAPTER 8

Gordon ran his tongue around the inside of his mouth. He couldn't taste vomit, nor did he have chunks of anything in his mouth. Which, he supposed was something. His teeth felt clean, like they'd been sandblasted, and his throat was raw when he swallowed. His head didn't hurt.

He opened his eyes, half expecting to be in the car, or in the street, or halfway up a church spire, but he was in bed. His bed. Relieved, he sat and looked around. Everything looked in place. "Okay," he said to himself, swinging his feet from the bed. "What the fuck is going on?" He got up. He was naked. He never slept naked. He pulled on a pair of shorts from the chair at the end of the bed and a tee. He padded along to the bathroom and looked in the mirror.

He looked God-awful. Dark rings sat under his eyes. He was pale. There was a crust on the inside of his nose where blood had dried.

He washed. Cleaned himself. He *had* been cleaned, even if it was rudimentarily. He wondered if he'd done it himself in some drug induced state—she *must* be drugging him—or if she had done it. She must be coming and going from the room at will, somehow. Without his knowledge. And probably slipping hallucinogens into, well, everything.

Either that, or she was some cosmic entity that had the universe inside her. And weird gelatinous goo. He shuddered remembering everything until he passed out. Gordon picked up has toothbrush and shoved around in his mouth for a few minutes, thinking.

The obvious answer was to finish with her. Just go and get a hammer and smash her fucking skull in. He'd just leave her to starve, but she must have a way out. Yeah, that made sense. Fuck her up. Clean it up later. Have a day off. He deserved it, after all, the hours he'd been putting in with her. Netflix and kebab. Or a Chinese. He dropped the brush back into the sink and grinned maniacally at himself checking his teeth … ran his hand through his hair, scratching at it. He sniffed his pits. Nodded to himself and left for the garage.

Outside, he could hear that dog barking again. He looked at his wrist—that was right, no watch. He had to find that. What time was it?

What day …? He squinted at the sky. Early morning. Real fucking early. Why the Hell was Nathan's dog out at this time? He always took the yappy little shit out when he got up—like most dole scroungers—around lunchtime.

He got to the garage door and stopped, his hand resting on the handle. Dog still yapping. "Look," he said to himself, "how much weirder can this week get?" He let his handle drop and walked down to the path, looking over to Nathan's house. There were no lights on inside. He padded, still barefoot, along to the gate into Nathan's front garden. The barking was coming from around the back. He opened the gate. A little creak from the hinge. He stepped into the garden and walked carefully along the path towards the house, letting out the odd *ow*, and *ouch*, as he stood on stones. He stopped. What *was* he doing? What did he really care if Nathan had left his stupid dog out all night?

Then he heard a bark a little closer.

Damn. The fucking rat-animal had heard him come through the gate and was coming around to yap at him. Before Gordon could turn, the animal circled the corner of the building. It was one of those light grey dogs. A cross something-something. He could see instantly that it had something on its face. Curiosity got the better of him and he crouched down, allowing the thing to approach.

Blood.

Of course. Of course there was blood on the dog's snout. "For fuck's sake," he said standing. The dog trailed around at his feet snuffling for food. Gordon absently kicked at the animal, and it scurried away from him. He noted that its lead was trailing behind it. Gordon walked around the back of the house quietly, and carefully. He wanted to have nothing to do with whatever was around there—perchance Nathan had a heart attack when taking whatever-its-name-is for a walk and the little shitdog had feasted on his flesh at the first chance it got—or, or, there was nothing more than a dead bird around there and Nathan had left the thing out all night.

Don't get involved.

Immediately it looked more like the former. Nathan was lying on floor by the back door. Gordons morbid curiosity had brought him this far, but Nathan drew him a little closer. If the shitdog had done this, it'd done a particularly good job, and perhaps Gordon himself might consider feeding the fucking thing. Gordon stepped closer. He just wanted to *see*. A mental picture that he could smile about later when he'd dealt with his own problems. Maybe have a wank to it. As he got closer, he saw that whatever had done this to Nathan had done it some time ago. The blood wasn't completely dried out on the ground, but even from a short distance away, Gordon could see the glisten of the liquid, still fresh enough.

But he wasn't paying attention and he realized too late that he had gotten too close. He kicked something that rattled across the path in front of Nathan, and he lost his footing, stumbling straight into the blood. "Oh, fuck no." He tried to keep it as a whisper even after the unconscious exclamation.

Bare foot.

Gordon looked at his feet. The blood wasn't viscous enough to bubble up between his toes, but lent itself the look of macabre foot painting. "Shit." He looked at what he had kicked to start with, that caused him to sidestep.

His watch.

He stared at the watch, and then to Nathan, then to the watch again as the cogs in his head turned slowly. When the penny dropped he looked skyward. "Oh, come on." Not only had been careless enough to contaminate the crime scene he'd just stumbled upon, turns out it was his crime scene to start with. He held his head in his hands for a few moments. "Think," he whispered.

"Right." Gordon surveyed the situation. *Ignore the blood*, he thought. *Get the body out*. Get the watch. Destroy the … he looked at the blood, and the surprisingly large amount of Nathan's guts that were on the outside … forensic evidence.

It was still early. He tromped through the blood, stepping on whatever was on the path and in his way. The intestines felt chilled on his toes. He stooped down and grabbed the watch, slapping it wetly back onto his wrist and fastening it. He scooped up the body in his arms—again, bride-like, he was getting better at the balancing act of the corpse-carry—and hurried as fast as his legs would carry him back to his own house. He was surprised at how much lighter Nathan was than he had expected, but that might have been his lack of insides. He was still heavier than the kid, though. He looked left, right, and left again as he reached Nathan's gate. There was a light on in the window at number six but no movement. Gordon picked up the pace and got the body back to his house.

He dumped it on the kitchen table.

If someone else discovers any of this before he had cleaned up, it was curtains.

He left the kitchen, back to Nathan's. Shitdog was taking a crap on the roses. Probably good for them. "Good boy?" He went around the back and started to scoop up Nathan's insides into his arms. "Damn it. Should have brought a bin liner." Did he even have any bin liners? Weren't they in the … oh, never mind. He got what he could carry. Ran back to the house.

He pulled the carrier bag of carrier bags that everyone's got from under the sink.

Back to Nathan's.

In the back yard he hurriedly pushed intestines

into Tesco bags, coming across the murder weapon buried under what looked like a kidney resting by the back door. He tossed it in the bag. Back to the front.

Grab the stupid shitdog.

Back to the house.

The kitchen now looked like a demented mortuary, crossed with Battersea dogs home. He shook his head, and went out closed the back door behind him. It was getting light.

Within maybe thirty minutes neighbours would be on the street, heading out, maybe pulling bins out to the path. Was it bin day? He rounded into Nathan's back garden and dragged the hosepipe off the wheel stuck to the side of the house, turning the tap on at the same time.

But he felt he had to leave the hose on the shower setting. Too much gushing water at this time might get curtains twitching.

Patter, patter, patter.

Gordon stood there like a gardener at the Chelsea Flower Show, heaving hard, exhausted with one hand on his hip, like this was the most natural thing in the world.

The blood turned to pink, dispersing slowly. Then came the shriek.

Gulls.

"Bloody hell." Gordon looked up and one was circling, shouting war cries and rallies to its fellow gull. The noise of the water had attracted them. Gordon turned the hose off. Finally, a stroke of luck.

The first one came down and consumed some of the gore far quicker than Gordon could have hoped to wash it away. *Huzzah*, he chirped internally.

He backed to the corner of the building, and they started to flock down like he'd just dumped a bag of day old fish there. He turned and fled to the house, as fast as he could.

When he opened the back door into the kitchen, shitdog was sitting in a coagulating pool of Nathan's blood that was gathering under the table. Gordon scooped the dog up. "You," he said, bringing the animal up to his face. "Are my alibi if someone asks any questions of the whereabouts of daddy. I'm looking after you, because Nathan was sick, and a family member came a took him away. Or something. We'll iron out the details later." He noticed a nametag on shitdog's collar. "Genevieve?" He looked at the dog in the eyes again. "And from this day forth, you shall be known as Shitdog. Better, right?"

The dog stuck its tongue out.

"Good enough for me." He put the dog down. "Now let's clean this place up."

He scooped up Nathan and took him down to the basement.

CHAPTER 9

Gordon regretted asking to watch.

Jane had opened herself again, this time as Gordon sat on the chair. He had his arms on the rests and his feet planted firmly on the floor in front of him. He was transfixed, and his body felt like it was trapped there, held by some unseen force. Nature itself sitting on his face.

The mess of Nathan lay crumpled on the floor in front of the entrance to the universe as insect-like creatures crawled from the space, from nowhere, creatures never before seen by human eyes—at least, eyes that would live beyond the sight—Hell's fleas, roaches perhaps, crawling over it. They were followed by what Gordon assumed was Jane, Jane in her real form. First came eel-like tentacles, tiny, thin, and slippery. They thrashed from one side of the gap to the other, feeling for the flesh. When they found Nathan they explored the corpse.

Gordon had done a good job on Nathan from the outset, and by good by good job, he nodded to himself, there was a somewhat out of character psychotic-ness to the damage that he had dealt to Nathan with nothing more than a knife. He had carved most of his insides about with the cleaver that he had found, again from his own kitchen set, outside Nathan's back door, most of it having been done after Nathan's demise. The massive head trauma, which caused the leaked brain matter was probably an early blow.

The eels squirmed over the corpse feeling their

way in and out of the wounds, snaking into a gash and out of the gape it left.

Then, satisfied that the flesh was there, or sufficient, or … Gordon didn't even know … larger tentacles came from the nowhere. Tentacles layered in rancid suckers, puckering like little baby mouths wanting to suckle on the teat. The girth of them was greater than that of Gordon's whole body, wider and more around than any living creature he'd been this close to before.

His head thumped with a burning passion, the pain behind his eyes getting bigger, pushing pressure at them, making them feel like they were going to explode.

Relax, said the voice in his head. It came from nowhere, and yet was everywhere.

Gordon could feel his blood pumping through his veins as the tentacles wrapped around Nathan's corpse, squeezing the juice from him, absorbing it, sucking the wet flesh from the bone, and the crushing what was left, to a mush, a pulp. Jane's tentacles reached across the floor, dissatisfied with the haul, looking, perhaps longing, for new flesh to absorb. More food. More nourishment. Gordon tried to move his feet, and pull them away from the feasting creature. "Jane," he shouted, knowing that wasn't her name, not when she was in this form, like this, some expansive entity.

His God.

As if she heard, though, the tentacles withdrew, leaving the eels behind, slipping through the blood on the floor, what was left of Nathan's clothes being discarded as they sought confirmation of the end of the flesh. Then they too were pulled back into the darkness by some unseen force.

Jane pushed, fighting her body back together, the slit in her skin rejoining as the body was made whole again, the impossible universe being folded away into her.

Gordon could feel his blood close to the surface, as if he were under some tremendous g-force, his own life trying to escape from his body, but the feeling eased as the universe was sealed. He could feel the pressure lower.

And Jane spoke, "Thank you for the flesh," she said, standing outside of the pool of blood, naked and unblemished as if nothing had happened.

Gordon realized that he was still breathing. His heart rate returning to normal. He could move his hands again, letting go of the arms like that first time he awoke, letting go of the steering wheel. He stood, shaky on his feet. "What are you?"

Jane smiled and returned to the bed, pulling the chain that still secured her to the wall, behind her. Gordon watched her butt. It was a good butt, whatever it was the butt of.

She sat. "I have no name. My kind have no name. We are they who have been here since before."

"Before what?"

Jane shook her head. "Just before."

Gordon walked from one side of the room to the other. He made sure that he stayed out of the circle of the length of the chain so she couldn't reach him, but he doubted that really mattered at this point. "I have no say in our relationship going forward, do I? You wear the trousers, right?"

Jane smiled. "You never had a say. Not after you brought me here. You should have let me get my business done."

Gordon frowned, "Why were you going to an accountants, by the way?"

"They made a mistake on my year end taxes."

Gordon shrugged. Made sense, he supposed. "So," he sighed and returned to the seat. "How much flesh? I mean, you're going to make me get it anyway, right? And you seem … less cautious with the whole *getting caught* thing. I mean, there's shitting on your own doorstep, and there's massacring the bloke next door. I would prefer not to go to jail for the rest of my life." He smiled and looked angelic. "And I'm sure you would too."

She half shrugged, which Gordon interpreted as either, *I couldn't careless*, or, *no, that would be terrible*. It could have been either in all honesty.

"I require flesh daily."

"Like, Nathan size?"

"Not like child size."

"Well, you made me get that one, I didn't have a say in it, but I'm going to need to take this farther afield if I'm not going to get banged up for it."

"Then do as you will to bring me the flesh."

Gordon nodded. "Right-o." He got up and opened the door. "Open or closed?" he asked.

"You may close me in. I am noisy sometimes."

Certainly when you eat. He smiled to himself. He closed the door, but didn't bother to bolt it, pulling the blind down to give her some privacy.

Halfway up the stairs to the hallway, Gordon considered how well he seemed to be taking all of this. But she did seem to have some sort of hold over him, an influence that went further than simple mind control trickery. She calmed him. Her presence made him not only understand, but accept her.

It was a strange feeling. Troubling. He knew there was a flesh eating God in the basement, and yet while there was nothing he felt he could do about it, he didn't really have a problem with it either. He … he just wanted to make her happy.

Pushing the door to the kitchen open, Shitdog came bounding up. It had been feeding on the flesh itself. Well, the blood anyway. "Whose a good …" Gordon stopped. He bent down and picked the dog up holding it over his head. "… girl?"

Yap.

Gordon put it down. He had twenty four hours to clean, and find tomorrow's … flesh.

Leaving the south coast was the only way forward. The nearest city was Ashbury, and that would have to do. It was large Cathedral city, and there would be plenty of pickings in the evening.

Gordon rumbled his fingers on the steering wheel. He was sitting at a roundabout just out of town. It was four-ish in the afternoon. It had taken him some time to clean the house up, and himself, and the basement. It was like he was *staff* all of a sudden.

Shitdog sat on the seat next to him. She wasn't strapped in, but she was behaving. Quiet, actually. He thought she might be able to assist. He had a plan for getting a hold of the flesh.

———

Gordon drove to a stop in one of the few parking spaces of the small public park that ran alongside the estuary that cut through the city. The rest of the spaces were empty.

The dark was starting to come.

And he felt … good.

The further he had gotten away from Birchingate, the better he had felt. The less … he stopped and thought about how he did feel. He felt more in control, more able to think clearly. It was as if the further he got from Jane the less of a hold she had over him. Clearly this could be a game changer. Now that he was feeling more himself, he could see that the hold she had made him feel things. Or *think* that he felt things, more accurately. She puppeteered him like a husband, and not like a slave. He *wanted* her happy. Gordon looked at Shitdog. He rubbed her head. "So we're going to do this? We'll swipe some flesh tonight, and make new plans after that." He couldn't just up and run. There would be too many complications. Mostly, someone would eventually break into the house thinking that something had happened to him, and find a naked God thing in the basement, probably very pissed off.

No, it was better that he do this the right way. Maybe brick her in and sell the house sans basement.

Either way, grab someone tonight. Get some flesh. He looked at himself in the rear view mirror. He looked rough. Like he hadn't slept for days. He was feeling so out of it as well. Like a lingering migraine was sitting in the back of his skull, and had been since this whole thing started.

He smiled at himself. *Charm,* he thought.

Gordon attached the lead to Shitdog's collar and the two of them got out of the car. The park was long and thin. At this end of it was the car park which led straight out onto the street, two minutes from the dual carriageway and freedom. At the other was the road that led straight to the city centre.

So he wanted someone from this side of the park. "Come on, girl." He gave Shitdog a little pull. "You're going to have to pretend to be Genevieve for one night. I'll get you a new tag at the weekend." He walked the dog away from the car park and onto the path in the park. A little way in he began to loiter. He wanted to look like his dog was the loiterer, not him, because he wanted to stay close to the car. This was going to take a little nuance. Style. And only a quick fucking bludgeoning.

He let Shitdog snuffle around in the grass for a while, staying to the trees, out of sight, out of mind. Nobody was going to pay attention to some likely looking geezer walking a shit dog at dusk. Once the light was gone, and there was less people, he waited. Watched.

He saw what he needed. A girl. Looked like a teenager from this distance. Skinny thing. More meat than a kid though. Gordon wondered for a moment where that first kid had come from, and then dismissed the thought, as no one had come looking for it. But it must have been local. Probably should check the local Gazette.

He bent down and let Shitdog off the lead.

The little thing scampered stupidly in a little circle and then started yapping uncontrollably. *Yap. Yap. Yap.*

"Genevieve," he called after her, half-heartedly.

The dog ran straight at the girl.

Score. Treats for you later. Gordon started a slow—almost pathetic—jog towards the girl who had stopped and was petting the dog. The old dog in the park routine. Never failed for picking up girls. Or so the Internet had told him. This was his first dog, and to be honest, it all seemed to be working out, so keeping her was looking likely. Especially if this had to go on for some months while he was selling the house.

He slowed as he approached the girl.

"Hello there, thank you." He bent in towards his knees and rested his hands down feigning tiredness. "She's a little go-er." Gordon looked at the girl for the first time, properly, this close. *Hey-ho. I bet you're a go-er too.* The girl was somewhere around eighteen. She was carrying a backpack over one shoulder—probably on the way home from uni or something. But who cared about that?

"'Sall right," she said, petting the dog as her tail went back and forth with enough gusto to take flight.

Gordon bent down and put the lead back on Shitdog. "I've been chasing her around," he said. "Thank you." He stood and looked at her for a few seconds without speaking. She turned away, embarrassed. Gordon looked around them. There was no one to be seen. Now was perfect.

He hated to do it, but needs must.

Gordon pulled the baton he had in his coat pocket and flicked his wrist extending it. She never saw it coming. He swung it with purpose. Hard. Bottom of the skull. Single blow. Never fails.

She went down like a sack of shit.

Gordon slid the baton back into itself, folding it away and slipped it back in his pocket. The pressure point at the back of the skull was always a winner—although there was a fifty-fifty chance that it might be fatal. He looked around the park again. Still no one. Thank God. He thought of Jane briefly, before crouching down and picking the girl up in his arms.

He really was getting good at this.

With Shitdog's lead wrapped around one hand, and the girl in his arms, Gordon started to hurry back to the car. He looked at her as he carried her, her face so close to his. She was beautiful. He lifted her up as he carried her, almost pulling Shitdog from the ground, getting her face closer to his. He couldn't tell if she was still breathing. He cocked his head. But did that really matter? He slid in closer still and stole a kiss. On the lips. She was still warm.

He felt a twitch in his pants.

Not now.

He got to the car. There were a few vehicles on the main road, but nothing too close. He didn't want to take a chance though. He leaned her against the car to help hold her weight and thrust his hand into his pocket, retrieving the keyfob. He unlocked the car and juggled the lead, the girl, the keys, and trying to get the boot open. Finally he got it up and dropped the girl in, slamming the lid and taking one last look around.

This was all too risky.

He wiped the back of his hand across his forehead, opened the door and letting Shitdog clamber in. Then he went around to the driver's side and got in. He was free and clear … this time … but anyone could have come up on him doing this. Curtains.

He started the engine and pulled out towards the dual carriageway.

As soon as Gordon got passed the city limits heading towards Birchingate, he could feel her getting stronger. He could feel her want.

Desire.

Gordon stopped in the garage that he had left open when he left, getting out the car and pulling the shutter down. He popped the boot open, and there she lay, unmoved. He reached down and rested two fingers on her neck. She was alive.

He raised an eyebrow, unsure if that made his lust stronger or weaker.

He took a breath and went out the side of the garage and to the rear of the house opening all the doors, before retrieving the girl. He took her and a knife from the kitchen to the basement, with Shitdog trailing behind.

———

The girl lay motionless on the floor of the basement between Gordon and Jane. Jane smiled weakly. "You are early."

Gordon hadn't even considered that. "Shit," he said. "Sorry." He stepped forward and crouched to pick the girl up. "I'll bring her back in the morning."

"What are you going to do with the flesh?"

He looked at the girl, and smiled. "I'll think of something."

"No," Jane responded quietly.

Gordon looked at her. It's not like they *were* married, it just felt like it in his mind. "Hm?" he asked, pretending some level of confusion or sudden deafness.

"You will not pleasure yourself with the flesh."

Gordon tried not to look crestfallen, but failed. "Oh, what difference does it make to you? I *deserve* it."

"You deserve nothing." Jane turned and returned to the bed, turning and sitting to face Gordon, her feet flat on the floor. She parted her legs, resting her fingers at the base of her belly, not *quite* touching herself. "You want what you deserve?"

Gordon nodded, his cock getting hard at just the slightest hint of the offer.

She closed her legs slowly. "Then you will behave," she said. "Take the flesh and wait until I am hungry before bringing it back."

Gordon dragged air slowly into his lungs. *Fucking Hell.* "As you wish." He picked the girl up and carried her out of the room, skirting by Shitdog. He carried her up the stairs to the first floor and into the back bedroom. This was all going to crap. He dropped her on the bed, looking at her with a level of wont, breathing slowly, surprised she hadn't stirred between the car ride, the carrying, the floors, beds. Maybe she was braindead. He stroked the front of his trousers. Maybe.

Anyway.

He should gag her and restrain her. He hadn't had to worry too much about such things since he built the basement, what with the locks and the soundproofing, but he was sure he could remember how.

He left the bedroom and returned to the

basement, giving Jane a little nod as he closed the door and dropped the blind. He didn't speak to her, he didn't much feel like it. *Bitch.* He went upstairs and returned to the garage retrieving some rope, a couple of bungees, some Gorilla tape and some superglue. He was sure that was all he'd need. He locked up and returned to the house.

In the kitchen he took a knife, and went back to the bedroom. She was still on the bed. He placed the knife down on the side table and the *kidnap kit* at the foot of the bed and sat three quarters of the way down it, near her knees. He rested his hand on her leg, uncomfortably at first. He shouldn't. Jane had forbidden it. But she wouldn't know, would she? Gordon could feel the girl's warm skin under his. It was the first time in a long time he could feel the difference between his hard calloused flesh, and another's, soft and supple. Youthful. He let his fingers meander up her skin under the skirt she was wearing. It was easy. A loose, flowing thing when she was standing, and now nothing more than a light summer covering. Hiding her modesty. The back of his fingers brushed lightly against her panties as he got bolder. He smiled. She was a good girl. Wearing underwear. Maybe a virgin? He withdrew his hand and bumped up the bed a little. Gordon slipped his hand under her shirt, touching her flat belly. It was rising and falling gently as she breathed, in time perfectly with her breasts. Rising and falling. He moved his hand up and felt the rib of her bra.

Gordon stood, excited. He fumbled to open his trousers, flicking the belt open and undoing the button. He dropped the fly and let them fall to the floor. He stumbled around, getting on the bed, getting over her, positioning himself to take her. So excited, as he was he didn't even remove his trousers from his ankles. It was lacking foresight, he released as his movement was restricted, but he was here now, and he wasn't going to wait any longer. Jane was never going to know. The girl would be dead soon. Pretty much a victimless crime.

Gordon held himself up on one hand next to the girls shoulder while the other ventured down to her skirt dragging it upwards and trying to pull her panties aside.

"Fucking Hell," he mumbled. This wasn't as easy as it used to be. When he was younger and this sort of thing was the normal Friday night routine he was … fitter? Maybe he should start jogging? Lifting weights? He realized how tight his briefs were, suddenly aware of how close to cumming he was.

Control yourself, man. He thought. *Dead nuns, Dead nuns, Dead nuns.* He managed to get his fingers inside her panties and pulled them to the left. Then he realized that her eyes were open.

She looked like she was about to be sick. Maybe just had been, in her mouth. She was wide-eyed, like so many of Gordon's other girlfriends had been, down in the basement. Something clicked in his mind that he hadn't gagged her, or restrained her, and this was … bad.

Then the warmth came just above his hip. Shit. He'd cum.

And then pain.

Tickling burning, turned to searing heat. Gordon tried to push himself back to kneeling, but the strength in his left arm was gone from holding himself up and he couldn't get the angle right for his right leg, like he'd just cramped. He rolled to the side, falling from the bed, clattering to the floor.

He flopped onto his back and lifted his head. The kitchen knife he'd left on the side table was sticking out of him, just above his hip bone. "Cunt."

He reached down and pulled it out, which in hindsight wasn't the smartest thing to do. Previously, the only other time he'd been stabbed was by a whore in central London, and she'd only stuck him with her Heroin needle. Again, he'd thought she was unconscious, when she wasn't, but that was another story. Blood spurted from the wound with surprising vigour. "Fucking Hell," Gordon exclaimed. He looked at the girl, who due to shock he suspected, had only just gotten to a sitting position. He slammed the knife into her side just below the ribs—which was as high as he could reach from his vantage on the floor. She screamed, but only weakly.

Gordon fumbled around getting to his knees, now easier without three inches of kitchen knife inside him, but still not easy because *his Goddamn fucking trousers were still around his ankles.* He still had a hold of the knife, and the girl had stopped screaming and was staring at him with her mouth open. A sort of, perpetual scream of silence. In fact, she looked like Munch's *The Scream*, come to life. He pulled the knife out and pushed it in again, near the same spot to the hilt, and yanked it downwards, hard. She started to gurgle, and then drew in breath, likely to scream again.

Gordon scrambled to his feet and pulled the knife

from her side, trusting it like an expert swordsman directly through her throat, skewing her like a bitch kebab. Her breath in stopped—mostly because the girth of the blade was blocking her airways—but she suddenly started to flap around like a deranged fish. She was grabbing at him, wild-eyed.

She was drowning in her own blood, *and* unable to breathe in because of the knife.

Oh, Gordon thought. *A twofer. Awesome.* And she was panicking. Gordon withdrew the knife again, this time causing her to cough up the blood from her lungs, but he could fix that. He put his hand on her forehead like he was going to exorcize her, and thrust her flat on the bed, drawing the knife back and pushing it up, under the rib cage and into where he assumed a lot of inside bits were that wouldn't benefit the addition of unexpected steel.

After, sixteen thrusts—or was it seventeen?— Gordon stopped, pretty worn out. She wasn't moving voluntarily anymore. There was blood being pumped from something, but it was being pumped onto the bedsheets, not around vital things. Like the central nervous system.

And she twitched occasionally. But he thought that was involuntary.

Gordon looked at the mess. *Well, this is going to take some cleaning up.* He looked at her. Her stomach and lower chest was a concave mess of innards, but her face was still intact, and her eyes open. If he shuffled to the side, she was still staring at him. He reached down, and found himself flaccid.

"Fuck."

Then, without the adrenaline required, reality crashed down on him like a 1940's comedy piano, and the pain in Gordon's hip returned. He flopped to the floor, unable to stand under his own strength, and clutched at the wound on his torso. "Fucking-fuck-fuck." He rolled over onto his side.

There was a lot of blood, and he had no idea how much of it was his.

He dragged himself across the carpet into the hallway. Easier said than done, and a good argument for hardwood floors in the future. Slippier, see? And also en-suite bathrooms. He pulled his way to the bathroom at the end of the landing by the bannister and into the tiled room, grabbing the towel that hung over the bath. He pushed it against the wound, and looked at the trail of blood that had followed him from the bedroom. "Fuck." He kicked off his *fucking trousers*, and reached down flailing about in his own blood, pulling his mobile from his pocket. He thumbed the screen and opened the browser.

Stab wound above hip.

He opened the first page on Google, which said *Stab wounds represent 88 to 97% of colon injuries in the civilian environment.* He wanted to read on, intrigued. *Later*, he thought. He flicked down the page, *blood source identification.* Why was it talking about arses again? *Right*. If there was kidney damage there would be blood in the victims urine. If not, it wasn't life threatening. Gordon looked at all the blood. *Not life threatening.* He shook his head.

He pulled his pants down and willed himself to piss. Nothing. *Try harder. Waterfalls, waterfalls, water ... sports. Damn it, concentrate.* A small amount of piss escaped his cock and looked at it. Brown-ish, no blood. It might be a bit early to tell, but clear so far. And he probably needed to drink some water.

He held the towel in place, and, realizing he wasn't going to die on his bathroom floor—body in the bedroom, God in the basement—started to laugh.

CHAPTER 12

Gordon had patched himself as best he could. Gauze and some gorilla tape—luckily the tape hadn't been used for any *other* purposes. He had slapped a bit of tape over the wound first … gorilla tape holds everything together, right? … and then gauzed it and taped it on, just in case. He had showered and tidied. The mattress was a right-off, and he'd have to decide on how to get rid of that later, the sheets and his clothes had gone into the wash, and the carpet had come up surprisingly well.

And he was done, by one in the morning.

He looked at his phone and wondered about having a kebab delivered, and then thought better of it. They got fucking aggie about delivering food much past one. He slapped his belly. He wasn't that hungry anyway, and was, surprisingly tired.

His head hit the pillow and he looked at the ceiling for a while wondering if Jane was going to leave him be tonight. Hopefully he was going to wake up here, unmoved from having no night-time killing sprees. He closed his eyes, and drifted away quietly.

———

The night was full of strange dreams. At first, he dreamt that he was out have fun, killing small animals at the petting zoo, but then they changed, he was a family man … married … had children, a job and responsibilities.

He awoke in a cold sweat. "Oh, dear God, no."

He swung his feet from the bed and looked at the time on his phone. Six hours sleep was plenty. He got up and stepped over the body wrapped in a tarp he found in the back of the garage, went downstairs and made coffee. He looked at the clock on the wall. It was nearly time for Jane's breakfast.

He stood, leaning against the sink and pulled his shirt up and lowered the top his briefs. The tape was still in place. He would tend to it later. Gordon swivelled his hips tenderly, and then retrieved two painkillers from the drawer and took them with the coffee. He mustn't let on what had happened to Jane.

She'd be pissed.

Gordon went down to see Jane. *Better make sure she's ready this time*, rather that, than carry the body down and then back up. He opened the door, having not bothered to bolt it when he'd left, and walked straight into Jane's real form. She was standing on the centre of the room holding her skin open, the void inside her, the universe, almost throbbing, tentacles out, in the room. The sudden pressure in his head was immense. He dropped to his knees, clamping his hands to the sides of his head, his eyes bulging, feeling like his brain fluid was punching at the back of them.

Then he noticed Shitdog.

The helpless little thing was encircled by the eel-like tentacles, wrapped in them, as she scrabbled against the smooth floor trying to get to get away from them, her eyes looking helplessly to Gordon as it tried to reach him.

"Noooooo," he screamed into the emptiness of Jane. "*Genevieve!*"

A puckering tentacle came from the black and plucked Shitdog from amidst the eels, and with a single *yap*, she was gone. Into the ether.

As the flesh.

The tentacles withdrew from the basement and while Gordon watched paralysed in pain, Jane re-assembled herself and then stood, waiting for him.

Gordon threw up over the floor in front of him. It was lucky he didn't have that kebab last night.

"Why?" he asked, raising his hand like he was posturing in some Shakespearian play. "She'd done nothing to you."

"The flesh," Jane said without moving, never breaking eye contact. "Bring me the flesh."

Gordon lowered his hand and sighed, the pain in his head subsiding enough for him to become angry. He stood. "Fine," he sulked. He had to keep himself in check. Make sure she still thought he was on side.

He went upstairs and scooped up the corpse in the tarp, before returning to the basement. "Here," he slung the girl to the floor, and the tarp opened, spilling her out.

"What happened to the flesh?" Still, Jane didn't move.

"What?" he blurted. "What was I supposed to do, buy her dinner?"

"You did try to fuck the flesh, so would dinner have been so bad?"

Gordon swallowed. "I don't know what you're talking about."

"I am inside you. I know. I know *everything*."

"Well." Gordon took a short shuffle backwards, trying to be as inconspicuous as possible. "I tried to be good."

"I know what you are thinking, and no, you cannot get away. I consumed the flesh of the animal because—"

"Of what I did to her, I know." He waved at the girl.

Jane twitched a small smile, and then it was gone. "No. I consumed the flesh of the animal because of the thoughts you had when you went to retrieve the flesh. Your plans to leave."

Gordon felt sick. *Shit. Think.* "I don't know what …" He let the words trail off. She had him bang to rights. Honestly, he didn't know what else to expect. "So what are you going to do because I did that?" He waved at the girl again.

Jane pushed her fingers into her chest pulling the universe open in a quick, sleek move. Gordon had no time to respond, and as *everything* became visible, her skin peeling back to reveal the blackness inside, his hands curled around his head and he screamed dropping to his knees. He was only inches from the tarp, the coagulating girl.

The eels came forth first as usual, slipping over the girls naked, split torso. They slimed around her, tenderly feeling their way across the flesh. Gordon watched. He was too close.

He could do nothing but pray that there was a God other than this.

Do you like? Jane's voice intruded his mind. He didn't want her there. He wanted to be far, far away.

Then came the tentacles, the monstrous arms of Gods, laying gently on the girl and then pulling her across the floor towards the edge of nothing. The eels, fought forward towards Gordon. He could watch them, but he couldn't move. He could feel the pressure of the blood circulating in his body too close to the surface, and he knew that he was squeezing his own head too hard. But there was nothing he could do, frozen in the presence of his God. The eels stretched closer, feeling out for him, forging their way to the flesh.

His flesh.

He screamed an empty hollow, silent, scream.

The girl was pulled into Jane, and the tentacles curled, waiting, waiting for the eels to find the flesh. And Gordon watched.

He could hear her silent laugh, nothing more than an impulse in his head, a voice free of the confines of reality. She was in him. She *was* him.

And then suddenly the eels withdrew, the tentacles slid back into the space between the universe and Gordon, with what little conscious thought he had left, watched—the girl was gone—and Jane rebuilt her skin in front of him, locking herself back inside the cage that was *her* flesh once again.

As the pressure eased in the room, Gordon managed to pull his fingers from his temples, feeling the bruising that they had caused already starting, and he slumped to his side, falling almost foetal on the cold hard floor, breathing like he had just finished a marathon, his head pounding.

She walked over to him, naked as the day the flesh was born. He was well within the walking circle of the chain, and she still had not removed it, although he knew now that she could have done anything that she wanted.

She knelt next to him and rolled him onto his back, leaning over him like an early morning lover. "You wanted to fuck the flesh," she said. It wasn't a question, and even if it had been, Gordon was in no mind to respond. He stared past her to the ceiling. Every inch of him hurt like he'd just surfaced from the depths of the sea too fast, and he was relieved. For just those moments, looking into the eyes of the universe, the heart of his God, he thought—*knew*—he was going to die.

Jane was undoing his belt and pulling his trousers down. She released his flesh, and without thought nor wont, he couldn't even feel it, he knew he was hard. She straddled across him and fucked him.

CHAPTER 14

Gordon looked in the bathroom mirror briefly, as he brushed his teeth. He didn't really care to brush anymore, but he needed some sort of pretence of normality. He looked at the bags under his eyes. He looked like he hadn't slept in a week. Maybe nearer two. He was thinner, too, that was for sure. Pale as a ghost.

He dropped the brush on the back of the sink and spat paste streaked with blood into the sink. He shrugged, not bothering to wash it away. He looked at his watch. It was nearly ten at night. The pubs would be turning out soon and he needed to find a fare. He was running out of ways to grab people off the street without getting caught. Fifteen and counting. Luckily they were all going missing, so it hadn't been until last night that the *spate of disappearances* had reached the news. It seemed the South East's boys in blue were less worried about people disappearing. No body, no foul.

That at least had bought him some time.

Returning to the ground floor of the house, he opened the door to the basement, and called out, "I'm going now. Back soon." There was no answer. There never was, but he wanted Jane to know where he was at. She might punish him if not.

He went to the garage and pulled the car out. He would go to Ashbury again. Jane was stronger now, stronger than she ever had been, and he could feel her with him like she was a passenger in the car.

Gordon listened to some light jazz on the drive. He tried to keep his mind empty. She knew what he was thinking most of the time, especially when his thoughts were strong, needy, dripping with desire. He could keep her out by not wanting the flesh. He could keep her out by not internally verbalising his thoughts. He could *feel* without her, but not think.

It made the process of getting rid of her extremely hard.

And he knew without her doing it that she could control him if she wanted to. If he were to run and she felt her grip loosening, she would just bring him back. He pulled into the taxi rank at the top of the high street. It was eleven-thirty. He needed someone tanked. It was easiest.

There were a group of three young men were coming up the street. Gordon looked down the line of waiting cabs. There were several in front of him. Good. He didn't want *them*. He pulled out his flask and poured himself a coffee, black, no sugar. He only drank it now for the sustenance. Ever since he and Jane, well, since she'd fucked him, he'd lost all but the very edge of his taste buds. It was a shame. He had missed kebabs this last week. He waited. A young woman was coming along behind the boys. Pretty. *Pretty fuckable*. No. He shook his head and looked the other way, waiting for her to get into another cab. It was best that Gordon didn't even look.

After another few minutes, a middle-aged guy came weaving up the street toward the taxis. He was pretty weedy looking, running his fingers along the shop fronts to try and keep upright. Perfect.

Gordon watched him go to the front of the line. He counted. There were two cars in front of him. He crossed his fingers. The guy went to the first one and there was an exchange of words. Then the bloke stumbled along towards Gordon. He looked at the driver of the car in front but then continued to Gordon's Mondeo. He leaned down, pushing his weight into the open passenger side window.

"Takin' a fare?" His voice was slurred, his eyes weak. He mouth hung open making him look like he'd had a stroke.

"Jump in the back," Gordon answered.

The guy fiddled with the rear door for a few seconds before managing the handle and then pouring himself into the back seat. He slammed the door. "Those cunts said I was going to throw up," he blurted, suddenly.

"Are you?" Gordon put his arm up on the passenger seat and swivelled to look at him. He smiled at the guy. "Nah," he continued. "You'll be fine." He turned back. "Where to?"

"Addington Street, just off Westgate Towers."

The other side of the city? Perfect. He pulled out into the dual carriageway before the fare had a chance to try and pull his seatbelt on, and took the forth exit on the next roundabout. "Heavy night?" Gordon asked.

"Hm." The guy's head was slumped forward and was lolling from side to side.

Watching him in the mirror, Gordon tried to work out if the guy was going to pass out, puke, or both.

Either way, he looked to be in just the right place for Gordon to move forward. Gordon pulled the syringe from the cubby in the door and just held it for a moment. He knew it was full, and that it would work, but just holding it made him feel better. More in control.

He pulled out of the bus lane and took a right at the next roundabout, pulling off the city wall circular and into the car park that the shoppers all used. It was empty. He pulled over, into one of the spaces, and quickly got out. He rounded the car. When he opened the door next to the guy, his eyes were open and he was frowning.

"This isn't home," he slurred.

Gordon leaned in close to him. "You looked like you were going to chuck." The guy stank of shit lager.

"Hm," he grunted, looking around, trying to get a baring.

When he was looking away from Gordon, he stuck him in the neck, pushing the plunger down hard. The guy let out a small yelp, and tried to reach up and feel where the needle was, but couldn't seem to get his arms up that high, whether from the drug, or from the drink. He wavered back and forth for a few seconds and then slumped down across the seats.

Gordon looked at the syringe with admiration. "Good job," he said nodding.

He straightened outside the car and looked around. The car park was deserted. He slammed the rear door and got back in the car, taking off for home. As he drove out of the city and into the quieter roads between fields, he watched the guy sleep.

His meal ticket out of there.

CHAPTER 15

Returning home, Gordon dragged the guy from the back seat and lay him out on the floor of the garage. Jane didn't seem to mind if the flesh was fresh of not. He chuckled. It rhymed. And while the guy *should* sleep until morning with that much Midazolam flowing through his blood stream, it was best not to take any chances.

He put down a tarp and rolled the guy onto it. He was wearing some thirty-year-old looking biker jacket, and a pair of fucking expensive designer jeans. Mid-life crisis drinker, for sure. Trying to re-capture his youth. The wife's probably just left him for a doctor—someone more mature and reliable, perhaps—and he was out trying to find a younger model, drinking heavily as the night drew on when he realized he was about as good a catch as an old tire. He looked at the jeans and tried to weigh the guy's size up. Too small, he thought. *Right*. He crouched down and opened the front of his jacket, taking his wallet from the inside pocket.

He found some notes, good, cards, no interest there, and a driver's licence. He looked at the photo on it. Goofy motherfucker. He held the card up and looked between the guy's face and the photo. "This looks nothing like you …" he looked at the name, "… Daryl Jenkins." He tossed the cards and the wallet on the tarp next to the body. "Daryl, motherfucker," he giggled to himself. He counted the cash. Nearly three hundred quid. Not bad for three hours work.

He winked at Daryl. "So, how do you want to

go?" He smiled to himself. "Quietly, I see." Gordon tapped his foot on the floor. "No such thing here, matey." He stood and looked around the garage. He wanted to inflict some … damage to the flesh.

Resentment was a strong word, yes.

And Gordon resented Jane.

The thing is, she knew it. She knew *everything*. At least she thought she did. If he turned up with pristine flesh she might suspect. She might actually *know* something was up. He walked over to his tool wall—a piece of ply he had attached to the wall of the garage and screwed a variety of hooks and screws in, where he kept some of his most interesting tools.

He picked up the plasterboard saw—a saw that looked like a machete, except it was viciously toothed, and sharp as fuck. He carried it over to Daryl, feeling the weight of the saw. "Not bad," he said. "Not bad." He crouched and lined up where he would cut. Maybe, hack the arm off? Hack all the limbs off? He shook his head. Too, melodramatic. Not like him at all. He returned to the wall and placed the saw back. He looked at the chainsaw. *Too noisy.* But a shame. He cocked his head at the sledgehammer. "Hmmmmm …" His hum went on for some time without him moving from the spot, transfixed.

He took the end of the handle in one hand and the middle in the other, lifting it from the hooks securing it from the wall. The weight of the metal head was imposing. It was a full-size version, with a four-foot handle. He'd gone to buy a stumpy one from B and Q, but the girl that was working the aisle was hot, so he ended up buying the biggest one.

He had never to this day found a use for it.

He stood over Daryl, wishing he were conscious. Just so that he could enjoy it a little more. He lined it up, and raised it like an axe in a film. The weight was grand. He felt … *Nordic* … and bearded. The head of the hammer grazed the ceiling, putting Gordon off enough that the sledgehammer came down mightily on the concrete floor next to Daryl. The sound reverberated around the inside of the garage bouncing off all the walls, back to Gordon and then off again. It would likely have been heard for some distance in the street too.

"Fuck." Gordon let the hammer go, standing proud with its head flat on the floor. He breathed in and out slowly. *In through the nose*, he thought. He took the hammer again and lifted it, his time taking the weight on his shoulder, holding it, preparing.

He lifted it again, swinging slightly lower to miss the ceiling and brought the metal head of the hammer down straight into Daryl's face. His head split like a melon, and then popped. Or exploded. It was hard to decide which. Brain fluid slashed like cum in a whorehouse, skull flew like boomerangs, and gloopy bits of Daryl's thinking sponge blobbed out like jelly.

And it didn't kill him, either. Well, not right away. The heart still pumped, blood chugging out of what was left of the throat-mouth bit, like someone had left the pump on at Tesco's petrol station.

It was the single funniest thing Gordon had ever seen.

He started laughing uncontrollably, leaning his

weight on the hammer like a cane. He looked around the room as his laughter subsided to more of a guffaw. There was fucking blood everywhere. Including all over his jeans.

And he didn't care a bean.

He dragged the sledgehammer to the side of the room and folded the tarp over Daryl, allowing the blood to run freely into the soakaway, or not, as it pleased. He shook his head, regaining his breathe. "Sick fuck," he said quietly.

He walked calmly back to the house. It was well into the early hours now, and the lights from all of his neighbours houses and flats were off. Inside he drank a glass of water, showered, and then went to bed. He set the alarm on his phone for five-thirty. *Hardly worth it*, he thought, before what passed for sleep these days took him.

A void of nothing without rest, taunted by Jane in the shadows and she poked his psyche, resting the body, but torturing the flesh.

CHAPTER 16

Gordon poked his mobile until it stopped beeping. *Stupid thing*. He got out of bed, rubbing his eyes. They were dry. His bones felt like they ached. Not his joints. *His bones*.

He had to keep his mind blank, as he had done each morning. Jane's presence was weakest after she had fed. Once she had taken the flesh and Gordon had left, he could feel a small detachment to her. It was like she was sleeping. Then, he felt that he was more able to do as he pleased, as long as he didn't focus on it too much. It was a strange sensation, going about his business trying not to pay attention to what he was doing. Each time he found himself concentrating on something too much, she got closer. It was like he was sneaking around her slumbering mind, trying not to wake her.

And he had to do it now, while she was awake.

He went down to the garage. The night had been unseasonably warm and the flies had gathered over the flesh. The smell was ripe. A mix between week old fish and shit. Gordon stepped around Daryl's brain bits, dried out on the concrete. He opened the door of the car and took out a roll of fabric, gently.

Not thinking about it.

He walked over to the flesh and knelt, tossing the covering from the body. Releasing the flies. He rolled the fabric open, revealing the seven syringes that he had created this week. Every day as she slept, he would fill one syringe with the hydrofluoric acid he had acquired from a local commercial cleaners. Just one though. Never doing too much. Never waking her. He filled the syringe and hid it away, tip toeing quietly in her mind.

And now he tip toed as he plungered the acid into the flesh.

One, two, take a break.

Three, four, do some more.

Once all seven had been injected into the flesh, he left them there on the ground. Nothing to worry about. Nothing to think about. He scooped up the flesh in his arms, a smile, as he briefly remembered carrying the flesh as a bride.

Time and again.

He'd become more than accustomed to his neighbours timetables now, as he freely carried the flesh between the garage and the house, leaving all the doors open as he went, in to the stairs to the basement and down.

The door to Jane's room was open now. There was no point in closing it. Neither of them held any secrets from the other—at least as far as she was concerned—and what little willpower he had left was hiding in the folds of his mind, plotting.

Kill the flesh. Kill *her* flesh.

It was the only answer he could see to escape this monotonous formula that could only end up with him in jail. In the beginning he had tried to explain to her that he couldn't keep bringing the flesh. It would bring others, but she hadn't listened.

And now it came to this.

He walked halfway across the room and dropped the tarp, the flesh, to the floor, and retreated a few steps. Enough that the eels could reach him if they desired, but close enough for him to watch. It was what she wanted. She derived some sort of sexual fulfilment when the eels slicked across him, and each time they fucked a little bit more of him left with her. A little more in the universe, less in his consciousness. He had to end it.

Jane stood from the bed and walked closer to the flesh. She smiled and parted her skin with her fingers and the universe revealed itself once again.

Gordon held his head. He could feel the blood coming from his ears quicker this time than last. He knew that his body couldn't keep doing this. It was breaking down from the inside.

The eels came forth.

Over the flesh.

Gordon showed no concern over the eels. Today they seemed content with the flesh. The tentacles followed the eels to the corpse, suckering against it, and pulling it towards the void. Gordon closed his eyes. He felt like he was crying, but he knew his eyes were bleeding. Each time, the pressure got worse, as if she was gaining power.

The body disappeared into the empty, and the eels retracted in with the tentacles. Jane started to pull herself back together. The pressure within Gordon started to lessen. The gash in her body started to seal from the belly up, reaching the space between her breasts when she stopped. He looked up at her.

He wondered if it was going to work.

As soon as he had thought it, he knew he shouldn't have, and she still had a hold over him. He couldn't stand. There was no getting away. He looked at her, as a single line of black liquid rolled from the top of the slit in her body and ran down towards her navel. She bled.

She didn't speak with her voice, her body, but inside his head. *What have you done?*

Gordon smiled. The question itself was enough for him to know it had done something. That it must be working.

Jane seemed to be struggling to push her skin closed, the ease of all the other times she had done it, gone. The look on her face was that of struggle. Gordon tried to stand, to get out of the basement. He needed to take this chance, whatever he could, to leave. If he could get far enough away …

The black goo ran from Jane's gash. "No." She tried to hold the skin together, but it tore, falling asunder as the acid seemed to burn it. "*You fool,*" she said. The skin she was trying so hard to hold together was blackening quickly, and almost dissolving away, black goo pissing from the wound, the universe being released. The skin on Jane's face started to sink, to melt from the bones, a whole in reality appearing in its place.

Gordon realized that what was inside the skin, the real Jane was spewing out into his world, no longer confined by the body. He pushed, trying to get to his feet, but no matter what was happening with the body, her mind was strong. Angry.

Jane's skin was pulled from the skeletal form it held, releasing black, tar-like blood to the floor. It dropped Daryl's flesh, half consumed by the cosmos, leaving it to roll towards Gordon, acid still eating at the raw flesh, and parts of him sucked on like a kid's lollipop with weird gelatinous substances slicking his body.

The universe slipped out into the room, darkness absorbing light. The room being lost to the void.

Gordon screamed a silent scream as Jane fucked him. She slid in and out of him, finding ways to intrude into his flesh, her life quashing his, his consciousness sliding away from him, trapped, motionless in a floating nothing as he became part of her.

C H A P T E R   1 7

Gordon opened the boot of the car and dropped the thin body inside. It slumped, lifeless, over the other two. Somewhere in the distance, beyond the flesh, Gordon could hear screams. It was hard to hear, trapped, with no control, no more than a glimmer in the body that used to be him.

He looked down at himself. There was blood on him. He held a screwdriver—one from his garage wall—and he tossed it in the boot next to the bodies. The top one moved. Just a little. From within where ever he was, Gordon could tell the child was alive. "Hush," he said. He wasn't sure if the voice was trapped in here to, or not. He slammed the boot, went, and sat in the driver's seat.

It was hot today.

The sun shone hard in the sky, halfway across the heavens. He wiped his hand across his forehead to push off the sweat, leaving a slick of blood in its place.

He started the engine, and reversed out the parking space. It was on the seafront, next to the beach. There were people running. They were shouting. Some were coming towards the car. Gordon waved like royalty and smiled at them, before driving out along the arcades towards the town.

He drove slowly, making sure that he obeyed the street laws.

Gordon pondered. What little there was left of

him was nothing more than thoughts. It was Jane that was driving. Jane that was killing. He was just along for the ride. A passenger. She was driving to the letter of the law. Like an old person. She couldn't have been more obvious if she tried.

The sound of sirens coming towards them caught Gordon. He still didn't want to go to jail, even if he wasn't in control. But maybe, just maybe, if he was taken far enough away she might lose her grip on him … but that was a hollow desire. He knew she wasn't going to let go. Ever.

The police car shot by, going towards the beach.

He drove around the churchyard, and onto the farthest end of Rochester Road, three or four miles from the estate, and waited patiently at the traffic lights.

Then he followed the line of cars away, along the road, towards Birchingate. There was an abundance of police activity, mostly going in the other direction.

He had passed by ASDA, and Tesco, and was passing Bean There when he noticed a police car following him. It was two, three, cars back. Probably returning to the station, but Gordon watched. He turned right onto the estate. His body was paying no mind to it. His mind raced as the squad car followed suit, turning onto the estate. "Jane, Jane." He had no idea if she could hear him, or if she even tried to. "The police, Jane. They're following us. You need to drive faster. Get away."

The car took another right into the close, drove quietly, peacefully, along to the house, and up onto the driveway.

Gordon saw the lone police car pull across the end of the road, blocking the exit.

"*Jane!*"

He turned the engine off and got out of the car. Several of his neighbours were there, watching him, watching the police car, confused. Gordon was bloody. They wouldn't be confused for long.

Gordon opened the boot of the car and scooped the first of the bodies up. Like a bride. The child was heavy, and blood pumped with some vigour from the screwdriver wounds. He probably wasn't dead still. *Yet*. He was heavier than he ought to be. Jane had made him take three children this time. Three, she thought, would be enough to sate her.

He turned and looked at the people in his street, standing, mouths-a-gape, watching him unload the bloody child like it was his shopping from Tesco. He waved a greeting, smiling, and turned, taking the flesh to the house.

Jane was all the house now.

Soon, Jane would be all.

T h e   E n d

About the Author

Ash is a British horror author. He resides in the south, in the Garden of England. He writes horror that is sometimes fantastical, sometimes grounded, but always deeply graphic, and black with humour.

Printed in Great Britain
by Amazon

21647006R00058